# Put Your Eyes Up Here
## And Other School Poems

by Kalli Dakos

illustrated by
G. Brian Karas

SCHOLASTIC INC.

New York  Toronto  London  Auckland  Sydney
Mexico City  New Delhi  Hong Kong  Buenos Aires

ISBN 0-439-68581-8

Text copyright © 2003 by Kalli Dakos. Illustrations copyright © 2003
by G. Brian Karas. All rights reserved. Published by Scholastic Inc., 557
Broadway, New York, NY 10012, by arrangement with Simon & Schuster
Books for Young Readers, Simon & Schuster Children's Publishing
Division. SCHOLASTIC and associated logos are trademarks and/or
registered trademarks of Scholastic Inc.

12 11 10 9 8 7 6 5 4 3 2          6 7 8 9/0

Printed in the U.S.A.         23

First Scholastic printing, September 2004

The text of this book is set in Barbera.

To my dear friend,
Jan Freeman Price,
for always believing in my
poems about school

—K. D.

# CONTENTS

## Introducing a New Me

There's a new ME this year,
An on-time ME,
A clean-desk ME,
A first-to-hand-in-assignments ME,
A listens-in-class-to-the-teacher ME,
A teacher's-pet-for-the-first-time-in-my-life ME,
An-always-willing-to-be-good-and-help-out ME,
A dead-serious-get-the-work-done-and-hand-it-in-
*before*-it's-due ME.

The problem is
The new ME
Is not like ME
At all.

## Give Me Normal

Ms. Roys met us
On the first day of school,
With a yellow stovepipe hat
On her head,
A skirt that stuck out
As if there were wires
Underneath it,
And black patent leather shoes
Like I wore in kindergarten.

She was waving
A bright yellow streamer,
And she yelled,
*"Happy New Year,
Penny"*
As I walked
Into her classroom.

"This is not normal,"
I thought to myself,
And sat down at
A bright red table.

Right over my head
Were dozens
Of giant inflated hands
Hanging from the ceiling.

Jennie leaned over
And whispered to me,
"She looks like something
Out of a fairy tale,
And what's with
All these hands?"

I started to bite
The nail on my baby finger,
Fairy tales, hanging hands,
And school
Don't go together
In my book.

Happy New Year, Penny

Give me
Normal and regular
In a classroom
And I'm happy.
You can even give me
Boring,
As long as I know
What to expect.

But,
Don't give me
A fairy princess
In a Dr. Seuss hat,
Wearing kindergarten shoes,
In a class
With giant inflatable hands
On the first day of school.

That worries me.
That makes me bite my nails.

# Ode to My Stress Ball

This spelling test I have to take.
I'll squish you in an ugly shape,

I'm tired of math and feeling blue,
I'll poke a hundred holes in you.

These compound words, I'd like to split.
You're one thing it's okay to hit.

My hands are bored; what will they do?
They'll make a monster out of you.

Oh, gushy, mushy glob of dough,
There's something that you need to know,

In school,
I don't know what I'd do,
If I couldn't play with you.

# The Hand Collection

During the second week
Of school
Ms. Roys showed us
Her *hand collection.*

She doesn't chop the hands
Off naughty children,
Or anything like that,
But she does have
A mammoth collection
Of plastic hands.

Some are bigger than
Beach balls,
While others—
Especially the pencil toppers—
Are smaller than erasers.

Some are pretty,
With long nails,
Others are slimy,
And one has fake blood
Painted on it.

She saves hands
For lots of reasons,
But I discovered
The most important
One of all
On the day Patrick was sick.

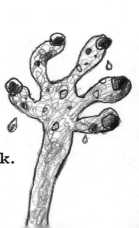

Ms. Roys has a weak stomach
So when
Patrick threw up on her shoes,
She gagged,
And threw up on Patrick's shoes.

Poor Patrick.
Poor Ms. Roys.
Poor class.

After school that day
I forgot my homework pencil
With the spider on top,
And had to go
Back to class
To get it.

Ms. Roys was
Sitting at her desk,
Patting herself
On the back
With a giant inflatable hand.

"I survived today," she said.
"And it was horrendous.
Sometimes you have to
Pat yourself on the back
Just for surviving."

"I remembered the pencil
That I forgot,"
I told Ms. Roys.
"Do you think
I could have
A pat on the back too?"

Ms. Roys laughed
And gave me
A giant green hand.

We stood together
Patting ourselves
On the back—

One teacher,
One student,
And six hands.

# Why We're Sitting at Our Desks Wearing Raincoats and Holding Umbrellas

Drip!

Drop!

Drip!

Drop!

In the middle of the week,

Drip!

Drop!

Drip!

Drop!

The roof began to leak.

# Before They Killed Her

When Ms. Roys passed out
The permission slips
For our field trip
To the museum
I checked her hands.
Because she bites her nails
Like I do.

She told us that she had
Fake nails put on once,
And after she chewed off
Three of the tips,
And nearly choked to death
On the fourth,
She had to remove them,
Before they killed her.

We all laughed,
And I liked the sound
So much,
That I'm going
To stop crying
About my
Chewed-off-to-the-skin nails
That look like
I eat them
For lunch,
And instead,
I'm going to write poems
And *laugh*.

## A Special School Lunch

BY PENNY

*Blubber mixed*
*With mashed potatoes,*
*Topped with*
*Penny's luscious nails.*

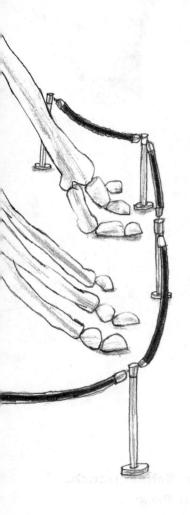

# Sleeping Beside a Stegosaurus on an Overnight Class Trip to the Museum

You were big,
I am small,
I am short,
You were tall.

You lived before,
I breathe today,
I walk the earth,
You died away.

You are extinct,
I hope I last,
I'm the present,
You are the past.

Your bones are here,
And I am too,
I am sleeping,
Right beside you.

You were wild,
And I am tame,
But something about us,
Is the same,
       the same,
          the same.

# In Color

I don't read very well.
I don't write very well.
I've never been the teacher's pet.

But,
Today,
Ms. Roys
Wrote a poem about
*Me.*

I've drawn
All kinds
Of crazy cartoons
On my bookbag,
And Ms. Roys
Says it looks like
An art gallery,
Right there
On my back.

She especially loves
My pictures of
Snoopy.

They remind her
Of her little dog,
Zoe,
Who died last year.
She says the cartoons
Bring back memories
That make her smile.

In school,
I've always felt
Like a black-and-white picture
That no one noticed,

But Ms. Roys
Wrote a poem about
*Me,*
And now I feel
Like I am filled
With pictures,
And they are all
*In color!*

# The Art Gallery on Penny's Back

BY Ms. ROYS

Penny is an artist and I love her work, I do,
Penny is an artist who makes
Special dreams come true.

Penny has the power
To remind me of the past,
Penny has the power
To make my memories last.

Penny has a gift that will
Bring both smiles and tears,
Penny has a gift she can
Share through all the years.

# Special Eyeballs

BY PENNY

The other teachers
Looked at me
And saw
A scrawny kid
With big glasses
And too many
Freckles.

But Ms. Roys
Had special eyeballs
That let her see
*An artist.*

## Why the Frog in Our Class Is Purple

We were painting
A mural today,
The frog got loose,
What else can I say?

# Worried About Being Worried

I'm so worried
About my spelling test,
That I'm chewing up
My chewed-up nails,
And my pencil
Looks like it has
A bad case of the chicken pox
And should be sent
Home from school.

Ms. Roys says,
"Relax
Your uptight muscles,
And then you'll do
Just fine."

My librarian says,
"Calm down.
Then you'll
Free your thoughts
To do their best."

My principal says,
"Don't worry
Your brains away
Like sand in a windstorm.
You'll blow the test,
If you're such a wreck."

Relax?
Calm down?
Don't worry?

Now, I'm worried
About being worried
About my spelling test.


## Our Teacher's Earrings

Two tiny lamps that give off light,
Two pencils long enough to write,
Blue toilet bowls that *really* flush,
We love her earrings—oh, so much!

# I Don't Believe in Ghosts

*Cast: Penny, Alberto, Ghost*

Alberto:   I think Ms. Roys is right
And this school is filled with ghosts.
Especially on Halloween.

Penny:   I don't believe in ghosts.
There's no such thing.

Alberto:   They float around all day
Right over our heads,
And sometimes
They sit in our chairs
And laugh when we sit down
On top of them.

Penny:   Are you dumb or what?
We *don't* sit on ghosts
In school.

Alberto:   They're everywhere—
On the ceilings,
The floors,
The windows,
The doors
Why, I bet some are inside
The desks.

Penny:   They wouldn't fit.

Alberto:  Yes, they would,
Ghosts can smoosh in anywhere.
And they can float into the gym,
And the cafeteria,
And the library,
And the bathroom.

Penny:  No way.
A ghost wouldn't be
Rude enough
To follow a kid
Into the bathroom.
I don't believe in ghosts even on Halloween.
But, if I did,
I wouldn't go
to the bathroom alone.
*Watch me,*
*I'm going into*
*The bathroom alone,*
And I don't plan
To see any ghosts.

(PENNY COMES OUT OF THE BATHROOM
SCREAMING!!!!!)

AHHHHHHHHHHHHHHHHHHHHHHHHHHHHHHH!
AHHHHHHHHHHHHHHHHHHHHHHHHHHHHHHH!
THERE'S A GHOST IN THERE!
THERE'S A GHOST IN THERE!

(Ghost floats out of the bathroom)

Ghost:  Stop yelling!
              Stop screaming!
                    Don't be afraid,
                          I'm here visiting,
                                My old first grade.

(Ghost floats out of the room)

Penny:  Ahhh!
              Look at my hands, Alberto.
              They're all white.
              I'm turning
              Into a ghost.

Alberto:  No you're not.
              You're just scared!
              Did ya see the way
              That ghost floated?

Penny:  Yeah, just like
              The special effects
              In a Halloween movie.
              And I could see
              Right through her.
              Could you?
              She looks real.

Alberto:  I've never seen anything
              Like it.

Penny:     Maybe our eyes are
              Playing tricks on us.

Alberto:   The school has only
              One first grade.
              Let's go and see
              If the ghost is in there.

(Penny and Alberto peeking in the first grade class)

Penny:     I see her.
              She can really float.

Alberto:   Yeah!
              She's floating over the desks,
              But no one is even looking at her.

Penny:     Look!
              Now she's sitting at that desk.
              The teacher and kids
              Are pretending she isn't there.

Alberto:   Maybe they can't see her.

Penny:     But we see her,
              Don't we, Alberto?
              Oh no!
              She's floating toward the door.
              Oh no!
              She sees us.

Oh no!
She's coming right through
The door.

(Ghost floats through the door and hovers above
Alberto and Penny.)

Ghost:     I always come back,
                 For a Halloween treat,
                     To my first grade class,
                         and sit in my seat.

                         Alberto and Penny,
                     With Halloween eyes,
                 You can see ghosts
             Farewell now,
         Good-bye!

Penny and Alberto:
AHHHHHHHHHHHHHHHHHHHH!

# When They Weren't Ghosts

When all the children
Go home,
Do the ghosts of the past
Come and sit
At our desks,
And write in our books,
And chalk on the blackboards,
And run down the hallways,

And remember . . .

*When they weren't ghosts?*

# Ghosts in Love

In the girls' bathroom
Under a sink,
Beside a gray pipe,
Someone carved
In perfect letters:

        Nathan loves Martha.
        Martha loves Nathan.
        June, 1934

When we told Ms. Roys
About this,
She crawled under the sink,
To see the carving,
And then two girls
And a teacher
Sat on the bathroom floor
And talked.

"I wonder who wrote
These words,"
Said Ms. Roys.
"Was it Martha,
Or was it Nathan?"

"I bet it was Martha
Because the words are in
The *girls'* bathroom,"
Said Meredith.

Then Penny added,

"I think
Nathan and Martha,
Are two ghosts,
Who must have been . . .
in love!"

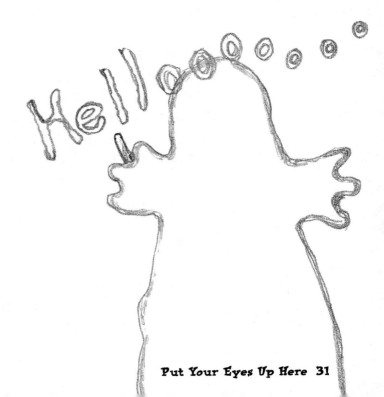

# Sometimes I Am a Ghost

Ms. Roys says
That every school
Is filled with ghosts.

"These are not the ghosts
Of dead children,"
She says,
"But the ghosts of children
Who have grown up."

I saw the ghost
Of my best friend, Joey,
When I peeked into the
Kindergarten class today
And remembered when
We were five years old.

Back then
We were like
Twin mittens,
Joined together
By a long string—
He was the right mitten,
And I was the left.

I could see us giggling
And squirting missiles
From toy submarines
At the water table.

Joey moved away
After first grade,
And it was the
Worst good-bye
In my entire life.

I've missed him
Every single day.

But whenever I peek
Into the kindergarten,
I see Joey,
And my five-year-old self,
And for a few moments,
*I* am a ghost,
Playing at the water table
With my best friend.

*Squirt!*

*Gotcha, Joey!*

# The Bell That Cannot Ring Is Ringing

The old-fashioned school bell
Was disconnected
Thirty years ago,
And now it cannot ring.

But sometimes
Ms. Roys says:

"Shhhhhhhhhhhhhhhhhhhhhhhh

The bell that cannot ring
Is ringing,"

And we stop our work,
Put down our pencils,
Become still as erasers,
And listen.

We *hear* it too.

Who is ringing the bell
That cannot ring?

Are they alive or are they dead?
Are they ghosts from the past,
Aliens from the future,
Or
Pranksters from the present?

So far,
All we have uncovered
Is the mystery
Of the truth.

*The bell that cannot ring*
*Is ringing.*

## When the Librarian Reads to Us

Goose bump good,
Goose bump good,
The stories she reads
Are goose bump good.

All over my arms,
The goose bumps grow,
For just a moment,
And then they go.

Goose bump good,
Goose bump good,
The stories she reads
Are goose bump good.

## My Underwear

In this classroom
There are twenty-three
Pink pigs
Pigging out on pizza,

And I'm the only person
Who knows
Where they are.

# A Cemetery for Pencils

I never thought a lot
About pencils
Until Ms. Roys
Brought out
Her pencil cemetery.

When I saw those old,
Broken-down,
Used-up,
Worn-out,
Pieces of wood and lead,
Pushed into
Styrofoam gravestones,
And read the book,
*Dead Pencils,*
Her students wrote last year,
I started to think.

Some pencils have happy lives
With good owners,
While others have tragic lives,
Like the poor pencil
That was chewed to bits
In my dog's mouth,
Or the purple one that fell
In the toilet,
In second grade,
Then got flushed away.

Cassie decorates the top
Of her pencils
With yellow, red, and orange yarn,
Until they look like
The wigs clowns wear,
And Billy likes to
Scalp the skin
Off his with a ruler,
And then laughs
At his "naked"
pencils.

I'm not
Laughing today.
I'm reading
*Dead Pencils,*
And thinking
About their
Tragic endings.

# Excerpts from Dead Pencils

## Your Resting Place
BY TAYLOR

Once you were bright, fiery, and sleek,
But a million numbers made you weak.

A zillion letters on the page,
Were enough to make you age.

I lay you in this inch of space,
Forevermore your resting place.

## Squished-up Pencil
BY STEPHANIE

Under a car, squished out flat,
Awful to end your life like that.

## Jaws
BY NICHOLAS

Your life was too short,
Because the sharpener
Demolished you,
Devoured you,
Destroyed you,
Gulped you,
In one trip
To its
J A W S!

# The Warm-up Test Before the Test

**1. Circle the right answer.**

    a)    a bug is a rug

    b)    a bug is a bug

    c)    a bug is a thug

**2. Fill in the blank with the best answer.**
An airplane is a _____ that flies.
(boat, train, plane)

**3. Are these statements true or false?**

William Shakespeare was a frog.     _____
Another word for duck is hog.     _____

A comma is a treat to eat.     _____
A lot of kids have two feet.     _____

The capital of France is Spain.     _____
You go to Mars in a plane.     _____

West is always facing west.     _____
You are ready for the test.     _____

# Put Your Eyes Up Here

**Ms. Roys:**  Put your eyes up here,
Put your eyes on me,
This way I'll be sure
Everyone will see.

**Students:**  We put our eyes up there,
We put our eyes on you,
You look like a creature
From an alien zoo.

**Ms. Roys:**  I look a little scary,
I really must agree,
With sixty eyes up here,
With sixty eyes on me.

# It's Snowing a Trillion Tiny Toys

**Students:**    It's snowing,
It's snowing,
The land is turning white.
Oh, teacher,
Oh, teacher,
Come see the awesome sight!

**Ms. Roys:**    It's snowing,
It's snowing,
A trillion tiny toys,
Go outside,
Go outside,
Quickly, girls and boys!

**Students:**    We're making,
We're making,
A giant igloo now,
We're loving,
We're loving,
This snowy day! Oh, wow!

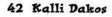

# Ms. Roys's Poem About the Snow

### You Melt Too Fast
BY Ms. ROYS

Snowflake,
Snowflake,
You melt too fast.

One second—the present.
The next—the past.

Like childhood,
Like childhood,
You go too fast.

# Children's Poems About the Snow

### A Pillow Fight
BY PETER

It's snowing,
It's snowing,
The land is turning white,
The clouds must be having
A pillow fight.

### Not a Single Sound
BY TALLY

Snowflakes flutter
To the ground.
From the heavens,
Earthbound.

### A Popsicle
BY PENNY

I'm holding an icicle in my hand,
It's a popsicle from winterland.

### An Awesome Sight
BY GREGORY

The trees are blooming,
Puffy-light,
Winter's blossoms,
Snowy-white.

### Delicious
BY TINCESON

The snowflakes twirl
North and south.

They glide inside
My open mouth.
Soooooooooooooooooooooooooo
Delectably delicious!

# The Hundredth Day

Ninety-nine days
Zip by so fast,
Sometimes I wish
This year would last.

It's the hundredth day!
We have a date
With floating pencils
To celebrate.

Amid gasps, shrieks,
Screams, and cries,
We can't believe
Our very own eyes.

A hundred balloons,
Or more, I say,
Are on the ceiling,
Bobbing away.

Check both your eyes,
Rub them again,
Pencils, markers,
Crayons, and pens . . .

Are floating in class
Bulletin-board high.
How did Ms. Roys
Get those pencils to fly?

The helium balloons
Have long thin strings
That give the pencils
Their magical wings.

We sit at our desks,
Stare up at the sight,
Pull down a pencil
And start to write.

To use a marker,
Crayon, or pen,
We reach in the air,
And take one again.

To let go of a marker,
Crayon, or pen,
We release the string,
And it bops up again.

"Pass me a red pen,"
Cries Joe to Sue.
"It's there by your head,
Bobbing right by you."

"Give me that pencil,"
Cries Bill to Jack.
"When I stop writing,
I'll send it back."

We work and work
And work some more.
Nouns and verbs
Are *fun* to explore.

"Just fifty questions
In math," cries Lou.
"Give us more work,
We need *lots* to do."

"I'll write a novel,"
Says Jennifer Lunn,
"So I can keep writing
And have more fun."

The whole day ends
In a minute or two,
And we're shocked
At the work we got through.

Ms. Roys is laughing.
"No homework today,
You've already done it,
Go home and play."

*Good-bye, balloons,
And a day so sweet,
Good-bye, Ms. Roys,
And your floating treat.*

# The Band-Aid Collection

Patrick is in love with Band-Aids,
He collects all kinds of them.

Big ones,
Small ones,
Fat ones.
Thin ones.
Nice ones.
Gross ones.
Round ones,
Square ones.

He has ghosts,
And scorpions,
And pink lips,
And dinosaurs,
And everything else you could imagine
On his Band-Aids.

He bought a Band-Aid in New York City
That is soooooooooooooooooooooo big
It could cover the bite marks
Of a brontosaurus.

Every day,
Patrick *wears*
Band-Aids from his collection
To school
On his arms,

And every day
We check to see
What kind of Band-Aid
Patrick is wearing.

Today we had to hand in
Our research projects,
And, of course,
Patrick studied Band-Aids.

But Patrick
Couldn't hand in his project,
Even though
He brought it to school.

I think the teacher
Will give him
An A+++++++++++++++++++++
Anyway—

From his forehead,
To his knees,
And right on to his shoes,
Patrick
Was *wearing* his research report.

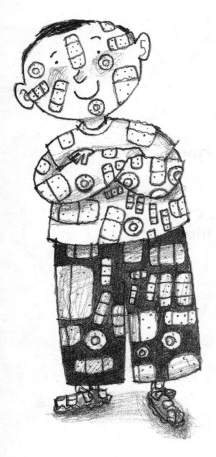

# Bugs Bunny Band-Aid

There's a drop of blood on Katie's knee,
She screams for Ms. Roys to see,

"My knee is bleeding hard and fast,
I'm going to faint; I cannot last!

"Call the doctor; call 911,
Oh, help me, help me, please, someone!"

Ms. Roys covers up the spot,
A Band-Aid hides the ugly dot,

But Katie sadly looks to see
A plain old Band-Aid on her knee.

"I'd like a picture or two,
This boring Band-Aid will not do."

Ms. Roys cries, "Oh, silly me!"
And sticks Bugs Bunny on her knee.

# The Magic Wand

Ms. Roys says
We all have magic inside.
It is our birthright.

One nose,
Two eyes,
Ten fingers,
Lots of hair.
Tons of magic.

On her desk is
A magic wand
To remind us.

Sometimes we borrow it
When we need an idea
For a poem or a story.

Sometimes we just look
At the colors inside
When it is all lit up.

Sometimes we hold it
And tell the class
About a special dream.

Sometimes we use it
To make a wish.

# Abracadabra

I need
I need
A break from work,
Before
Before
I go berserk.

I wish
I wish
A magic wand
Would take
Would take
Me to the pond.

I'd swim
I'd swim
The day away,
And then
Oh, then
I'd get to play.

I'll say
I'll say
A little spell,

*Abracadabra*

It worked!
It worked!
The recess bell!

## What Will I Do?

My lightbulb pencil is the best—
Saves my life when I take a test.

Math is easy as one, two, three,
When that pencil does it for me.

I win awards and make straight A's—
I'm the smartest kid in *all* the grades,

I draw like a wizard in art class,
And wonder, how this came to pass.

How did I go from the worst to the best,
From last in the class to ahead of the rest?

But then I worry, wonder, and fret,
And scratch a rash for I'm so upset.

It's the pencil, it's really not me,
That knows how to spell *geometry.*

It's the pencil, it's really not me,
That can add to a trillion and three.

It's the pencil, it's really not me,
That draws like an artist perfectly.

**BUT** even pencils with magical powers
Have to be sharpened every few hours.

When the lead is gone,
    And the magic is through,
        Oh, lightbulb pencil,

*What will I do?*

# The Shadow by the Classroom Wall

I am the shadow
By the classroom wall,
I am watching you,
And I know it all.

Don't try to run
Or hide from me,
There isn't a thing
I cannot see.

Don't cheat on a test,
Or lie to a friend,
I know the truth,
From beginning to end.

I am the shadow
By the classroom wall,
I'm watching you,
And I know it all . . .

And I know it all.
And I know it all.

I'm watching you,
And I know it all.

## Don't Go Near It

Margie the Mouse
Sits beside me.
We call her a mouse
Because she hardly ever talks,
And when she does,
It is just a tiny, tiny, whisper.

Yesterday she brought
A tiny magic wand,
With a hundred sprinkles
Of silver all over it
To school.

It looked like someone
Had taken the stars from the sky,
And pasted them on the wand.

She warned,
"This wand is small
And looks pretty,
But it is *dangerous*,
Don't go near it!"

The Mouse sits beside me,
And right in the middle
Of our spelling sentences,
When she was concentrating
On her work,
I watched my hand

Reach into her desk
And take that wand.

"I don't believe
In silly magic wands,
And I certainly
Don't believe
That *this* tiny wand
Is dangerous,"
I said to myself,
Hiding it in my lap.

"Ms. Roys believes
In magic,
And so does Margie.
But I don't,
And I can prove it,
With a magic spell
That *won't* work."

*Take this awful*
*Spelling away,*
*And turn me*
*Into a pig today.*

WHAM!
KA-BANG!
KA-BOOMERANG!
I'M FLYING!
WHIZZING!
SOARING!

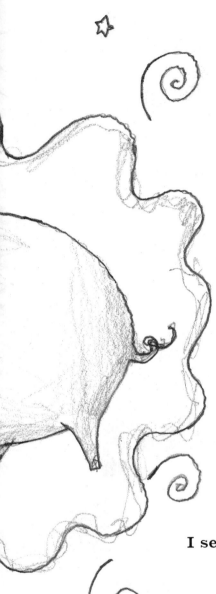

I WANT TO STOP!
I CAN'T STOP!
I'M CHANGING!
MORE LEGS!
SNOUT!
FUNNY SOUNDS!
FLYING!
WHIZZING!
SLOWING DOWN!
STOPPING!
STOPPING!
STOPPED!

Fuzzy eyes.
Wobbly legs.
Feeling strange.

I hear Margie yelling,
"Look, Ms. Roys.
I warned Penny
About that wand.
She shouldn't have taken it
From my desk!"

I see Ms. Roys looking at me.
I need to ask a question.

Mouth opens.

*"Oink! Oink! Oink! Oink!"*

# The Hand That Shook the Author's Hand

Yesterday, when
The Author
Visited our school
He shook
My best friend's hand.

Then
She shook my hand.

Please
Dooooooooooooooooooooooon't
*Touch* the hand
That shook the hand
That shook
The Author's hand.

Kalli Dakos

# A Gift for Ms. Roys

**Penny:** The end of the year is coming.
We need to find
The perfect present
For Ms. Roys.

**Brian:** My dad always gets
My mom flowers.

**Tally:** Boring!
Boring!
Ms. Roys likes crazy things,
Like walking hands,
And floating pencils.
It *has* to be crazy!

**Susan:** What about something
Crazy to eat?

**Jose:** We could buy her
Chocolate-covered spiders.

**Patrick:** Ms. Roys has
A weak stomach.
The spiders would probably
Make her puke.

**Fred:** I know!
I know!
The best idea
Is in my dad's beauty shop!

Penny: Like what?
A new hairdo?
A comb that talks?
A brush that walks?

Fred: Like fake fingernails
On a stick.
You know how Ms. Roys
Is always biting
Her fingernails?
Well, we could polish
Ten loooooooooooooooooooooooong nails,
In all different colors,
Put them on sticks
And make a bouquet
Of nails.
My dad has one
In the beauty shop
And it's really neat.

Penny: That's ridiculous!

Jennifer: That's goofy!

Brian: That's nutso!

Fred: Ridiculous,
Goofy,
Nutso makes it
    *The perfect gift!*

# Fingernails on a Stick

Fingernails on a stick,
Colored nails, long and thick.

For our teacher, Ms. Roys,
From this year's girls and boys.

You bite your nails, under stress,
You've chewed them off, more or less.

Ten perfect nails, long and neat,
Luscious nails, such a treat.

A good-bye gift for you, Ms. Roys,
*Thanks for sharing all your toys!*

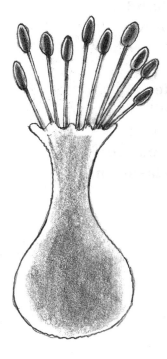

# A Good-bye Note to Ms. Roys

Dear Ms. Roys,
If you had come to school,
With pink and purple
Polka dots
All over your face,
Talking in Turkish,
And eating a
Pumpkin-size apple,
I wouldn't have been
Surprised.

At first I was afraid
Of your costumes,
And pencil cemeteries,
And inflatable hands,
And I didn't believe
In your wands,
And ghosts,
But after a while,
I'd race to school
To see what kind of
Mixed-up crazy magic
I'd find in our classroom.

No matter what happens
In my entire life,
I'll never forget
The teacher
Who waved a magic wand
In a boring old classroom,
And let us travel
On stardust.

       Love, Penny

## Forevermore

Let the other kids
    Go out the door,
       But I'll stay here,
Forevermore,

With Ms. Roys
And her Toys.